Let your smile change the world,
but never let the world
change your smile. —SJ and DW

For the first person to read children's books
to me, probably when I was still in the womb,
my precious mom. —CC

For Carla. —CD

THE TRUE ADVENTURES OF
ESTHER the WONDER PIG

BY Steve Jenkins, Derek Walter, and Caprice Crane

ILLUSTRATED BY Cori Doerrfeld

LITTLE, BROWN AND COMPANY

NEW YORK   BOSTON

ESTHER was a little piglet. She was rescued when she was six weeks old and arrived in a laundry basket, nestled among some towels.

When she looked up at her dads with those eyes and that smile . . .

. . . it was LOVE.

Esther moved into a little house with two dogs and two cats. She was the smallest of the bunch. (She was supposed to be a miniature pig, after all.)

Her dads didn't know much about mini pigs, so they had to learn quickly.

At night, everyone slept in his or her own
bed. Esther slept in a collapsible cat house.

But three days later,
she outgrew it.

So she climbed on top of the cat house.
That seemed fine for a while.

But then she outgrew that.

So Esther's dads got her a dog bed.

And then a BIGGER dog bed.
Her dads were confused.
"We thought she was supposed to be a MINI pig," they said.

But when she looked up at her dads
with those eyes and that smile . . .

. . . it was LOVE.

Esther liked to play outside in the pond.
She splashed around and flipped over the rocks.
She didn't mean to, but she scared the fish!

Esther also liked to help her dads with their gardening.

She dug up the bed, uprooted the tulips, and ate all the bulbs. (They were delicious!)

When Esther's dads saw the mess she'd made, they weren't very happy. But Esther looked up at her dads with those eyes and that smile...

... and it was LOVE.

Esther had the most fun at bath time.
She just loved to get everything wet. (She
even knew how to make her own bubbles!)

As she grew bigger, so did her splashes!

Sometimes, when her dads weren't looking, Esther sneaked into the kitchen and stole snacks.

She got into the freezer and ate all the ice pops.

She used her snout to open the cabinets and ate all the cookies.

Once, she even broke the door off the oven. (That was not on purpose.)

Esther's dads did not like this at all. But when she
looked up at her dads with those eyes and that smile ...

... it was LOVE.

Esther kept GROWING
and GROWING.
And GROWING.

So she started sleeping on a kids' mattress. Surely that would be big enough.
But it wasn't. She OUTGREW that, too!

Then she got a single bed.
And then a twin bed.

And then she even
got her own bedroom!

The little house was starting to feel very crowded.
What was comfortable for two dads, two dogs, and two cats . . .

. . . was way too small for a six-hundred-pound pig.

So Esther's dads did the only
thing they could think of....

They moved to a big farm where there was lots of room. (And where they could rescue even MORE animals!)

Even in a big brand-new home, everyone would gather together to tell stories or watch TV. But sometimes Esther would spread across the couch, and nobody else had a comfortable place to sit.

But when Esther looked up at her dads with those eyes and that smile . . .

. . . it was LOVE.

Then one day, Esther was not in her room.

She wasn't in the kitchen, and she wasn't in the garden.

Esther's dads searched the whole house, but their pig was missing!

They were SO worried. They ran all over the neighborhood searching for her. But she was nowhere in sight.

So what if she was so much bigger than they'd expected?
So what if she outgrew her beds in record time?
So what if she scared the fish, or ruined the garden?

She was their girl. She was part of the family. And families come in all shapes and sizes.

After hours and hours, a neighbor called out from her front door.

"Excuse me. Are you missing a pig?" the kind lady asked.

With great relief, Esther's dads followed the lady into her backyard, where Esther was happily eating all the apples she could reach.

"We're so sorry," Esther's dads said to the kind lady. "She's a very naughty pig." But Esther looked up at her dads with those eyes and that smile . . .

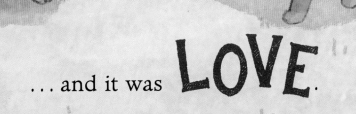

... and it was **LOVE**.

(But from then on, Esther's dads made sure their front gate was locked.)

THE TRUE STORY OF
ESTHER the WONDER PIG

In the summer of 2012, Steve Jenkins and Derek Walter really did adopt Esther, thinking she was an adorable mini pig.

She *is* adorable, but there's nothing mini about her. Even though her dads were told she would be fine in a normal house, after three years of growing, Esther weighs in at around 650 pounds—that's about as heavy as a female polar bear.

Steve and Derek bought a farm and opened the Happily Ever Esther Farm Sanctuary, where they live today. On the farm, Esther has plenty of space to roam comfortably. She spends her days rolling in mud, playing dress up, and hanging out with her animal friends—many of which were also rescued by Steve and Derek—including dogs, chickens, and a duck named Moby.

You can see more of Esther's life at estherthewonderpig.com.

Peace. Love. Esther.

The illustrations for this book were done in digital paint. This book was edited by Mary-Kate Gaudet and designed by Rae Ann Spitzenberger with art direction from Jen Keenan. The production was supervised by Erika Schwartz, and the production editor was Jen Graham. The text was set in ATAdminister, and the display type is Mark-New.